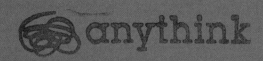

My Little Small

www.enchantedlion.com

First English-language edition published in 2018 by Enchanted Lion Books
67 West Street, 317A, Brooklyn, NY 11222
Copyright © 2014 for the text by Ulf Stark
Copyright © 2014 for the illustrations by Linda Bondestam
Copyright © 2018 by Annie Prime for the English-language translation
Original edition published as "Min Egen Lilla Liten" by Schildts & Söderströms
This edition published by agreement with Ulf Stark, Linda Bondestam,
and Elina Ahlback Literary Agency, Helsinki, Finland
A CIP record is on file with the Library of Congress
ISBN 978-1-59270-209-1

Printed in China by RR Donnelley Asia Printing Solutions Ltd.

My Little Small

Ulf Stark   Linda Bondestam

Translated from the Swedish by Annie Prime

ENCHANTED LION BOOKS
NEW YORK

In a mountain, deep in a cave,
in the dark, there lives a Creature.
The sun hurts her eyes and her skin, too.

If she were to go outside in the daylight,
she would feel a little sick. Then very sick.
Then she would die.

So she stays inside and, like the mountain,
is gray, gray, gray.

During the day, she watches the shadows slide
along the walls of her cave as she tries to sleep.
"It's the same outside," she muses.
"Gray, gray, gray."

She counts her fingers and toes to fall asleep.
When she's done, she sucks her thumb.
"Go to sleep," she tells herself.

Sometimes she dreams of the moon and of
having someone small to sing to and care for.

At other times, she wakes up crying
and whispers, "There, there. A big
thing like you shouldn't get so upset."

Then she sings a little song—
GRRR—to make herself feel sleepy.
If she still can't sleep, she gets grumpy
and pounds her fists on the walls,
causing rocks to crumble.

Sometimes she grinds the rocks
between her teeth:

KRRR, TFFT, FRRRP!

Then she rinses her mouth out with water,
and she feels a little better.

When dusk falls, it is time to go outside.
From the far side of the mountain,
she watches the sun set. The clouds turn lilac
and pink. She sees trees, houses, and the sea.

"How beautiful it is!" she thinks.

Then night comes.

Sometimes the moon is just a crescent.
But when it is whole and round, it floats
on the water. Once she swam to it and
threw her arms around it.
"Dear little thing," she whispered.
But it shattered into a thousand gleams.

How the frogs laughed at the poor Creature,
whose tears made the sea even wetter.

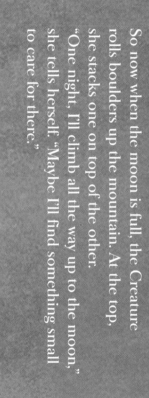

So now when the moon is full, the Creature
rolls boulders up the mountain. At the top,
she stacks one on top of the other.
"One night, I'll climb all the way up to the moon,"
she tells herself. "Maybe I'll find something small
to care for there."

But the boulders always roll back down
the mountain, knocking against each other
in a shower of sparks.

The Creature sinks down.
She gazes up at the stars.
"Don't be sad," she says. "You are big,
and everything will be better tomorrow."

Then she busies herself blowing spit bubbles,
which float high above the trees, shimmering
like milk in the moonlight.

GRRR, she sings, and new bubbles sail off,
small spheres of song.

One morning, something bright comes flying
into her cave.
A sun spark!
It hovers before plummeting
straight to the ground.

Viiliiii , squeals the Spark in a little flea voice.
"It's my only day on earth and I end up here,
where it is too dark to live!"

"But I live here," says the Creature.

The Spark shines so brightly that the Creature
has to squint. But it is small and can talk.
The Creature's heart starts pounding.
"Here is someone I can care for," she thinks.
And she asks:
"Will you be my very own Little Small?"

The Spark looks up and squeals again.
"Why do you squeal?" asks the Creature.
"Am I so very ugly?"
"So big and wrinkly," says the Spark.

A tear falls from the Creature's eye.

"Leave me be!" the Spark squeals again.
"Are you going to damp me down or snuff
me out?"

"Oh, no," says the Creature. "I'm going to
care for you for a thousand million years."

"But I can only live for a single day."

The Creature wants to hug the Spark,
but it would hurt her. So she lifts
the Spark up in her hand instead.

"There, there," she says. And she thinks,
"My very own Little Small."

The Creature says to the Spark,
"Where do you come from?"

"From the Sun," says the Spark.
"She is big and hot,
heavy and very clever."

The Creature feels a pang of jealousy.
Why does the Spark have to praise
the sun so much?

"Does the sun sing?" asks the Creature.
"Does she grind stones between her teeth?"

"No, but she creates color when she shines.
Why don't you go out into the light?"

"Because first I would feel sick.
Then I would die.
But please, Little Small,
tell me about the sun's colors instead."

So the Spark does just that,
shining her light first on a leaf.

"Do you see?" she asks. "The colors
are green, red, yellow, and brown."

"It's so beautiful," the Creature sighs.
"Tell me more. Tell me what it looks like
outside when the sun is shining."

So the Spark tells her all about the vast,
blue ocean, with its wonderful waves,
fish, and boats.

And she describes the hot, yellow, empty desert.

"Does anyone live there?" asks the Creature.
"Yes," says the Spark. "Some do."

"What else is there?" the Creature asks.

"There are forests that whisper when the wind blows, and grass that is green, green, green."

"Oh," says the Creature.
"I've heard that whisper.
But what about the other things,
the ones that can move
and jump, run and flutter?"

Sock Creeper

So the Spark tells the Creature about the
animals that jump and hop and climb.

Big Hopper

Spotty Runner

Forest Stag

Hidey-hide

Tree Hugger

Gangle-leg

Tiny Thing

Tree Swinger

Green Muzzle

Little Hopper

Gaudy Ground-pecker

And about the different birds that fly through the air.

The Creature closes her eyes and smiles.
Now she can imagine the whole world.
She can even see small things, like
dragonflies, beetles, and dandelions,
bright and yellow as the harvest moon.

The Creature feels happy, so she begins
to tell stories too. She tells the Spark
about the boulders she stacks up high.

"One night, we'll climb up the mountain,"
she says. "I'll carry you the whole way."

"I won't be here at night," says the Spark.
"I am only here today."

The Creature doesn't listen.
"I'll sing to you," she says.

She sings as sweetly as she can:

GRRRRRRR
GRRRRRRR

Soon her R's become as round
as droplets, falling on the grass
with tenderness,
like a gentle spring rain.

The Spark's glow is fainter now,
and redder. The Creature stops singing.
"Are you sick?" she asks.

"It is late," gasps the Spark. "Your singing
made me forget. I must return to the Sun
before dark. All little sparks must."

"I will carry you there," says the Creature. She hurries to the far side of the mountain, where the sun still shines high above the trees.

She blows a bubble around the Spark.

"Goodbye, my Little Small."
"Goodbye, Big Gray."

Then she blows the bubble away.
She hears a little GRR coming
from the bubble as it floats off,
like a little red star towards the Sun,
where it is welcomed.

The Creature covers her eyes,
to better see all the colors
the Spark lit up inside of her.

GRR

On her way home, the Creature picks up a sun-warmed stone.
She holds it gently in her hand, like an egg.